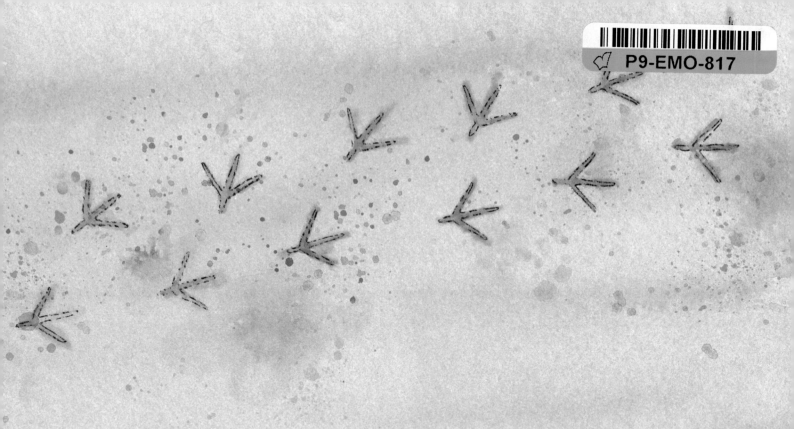

Janie Bynum ~~pecks~~ writes and ~~scratches~~ illustrates books in her southwest Michigan studio and also while she travels. Like Baby Chick, she was the youngest and chattiest sibling who had a habit of finding and bringing home friends of various species.

Janie has a BFA in graphic design with an emphasis on illustration. Her work has been recognized as a Junior Library Guild Selection. Visit janiebynum.com for more information.

For Oliver, who always listened. — JB

Distributed in the United States by NorthSouth Books, Inc., New York 10016.
Library of Congress Cataloging-in-Publication Data is available.
ISBN: 978-0-7358-4409-4
Printed in Germany
1 3 5 7 9 · 10 8 6 4 2
www.northsouth.com

FSC
www.fsc.org
MIX
Paper from responsible sources
FSC® C043106

Chick Chat

Janie Bynum

North
South

peep?

Baby Chick has a lot to say.

PEEP.
PEEP.
PEEP.
Peep!
Peep.
Peep.
Peep.
Peep.
Peep.

Peep. Peep. Peep?

"I'm too busy to chat," clucked Mama.
"Talk to Papa."

"Not now. I'm working,"
crowed Papa. "Talk to Sister."

"Maybe later," squawked Sister.
"Go play."

But Baby Chick has a lot to say.

So Baby Chick chatted alone.

The big round egg didn't answer.

The big round egg still didn't answer.

Baby Chick couldn't leave
the big round egg all alone.

peep.

"Baby Chick, is that an egg in your wagon?" squawked Sister.

"Baby Chick, where did you get that egg?" crowed Papa.

"Baby Chick, that's not your egg," clucked Mama. "Put it back, please."

Baby Chick tried to explain.

peep- PEEP- peep- PEEP- PEEP- peep- PEEP!

Baby Chick took the big round egg back.

Baby Chick kept the
big round egg safe,

peep!

and warm, and up-to-date on
barnyard news . . .

PeeP! PeeP. PeeP. PeeP.
PeeP. PeeP. PeeP.
PeeP. PeeP.
PeeP. PeeP.
PeeP!

. . . until Baby Chick was peeped out.

Let's hit the hay, Baby Chick.

Not even a peep?

Peep! Peep. Peep. Peep. Peep.
Peep. Peep.
Peep. Peep. Peep. Peep. Peep. Peep.
Peep. Peep.
Peep. Peep. Peep. Peep. Peep.
Peep. Peep. Peep! Peep.

Baby Chick woke up with a lot to say.

But the big round egg was gone.

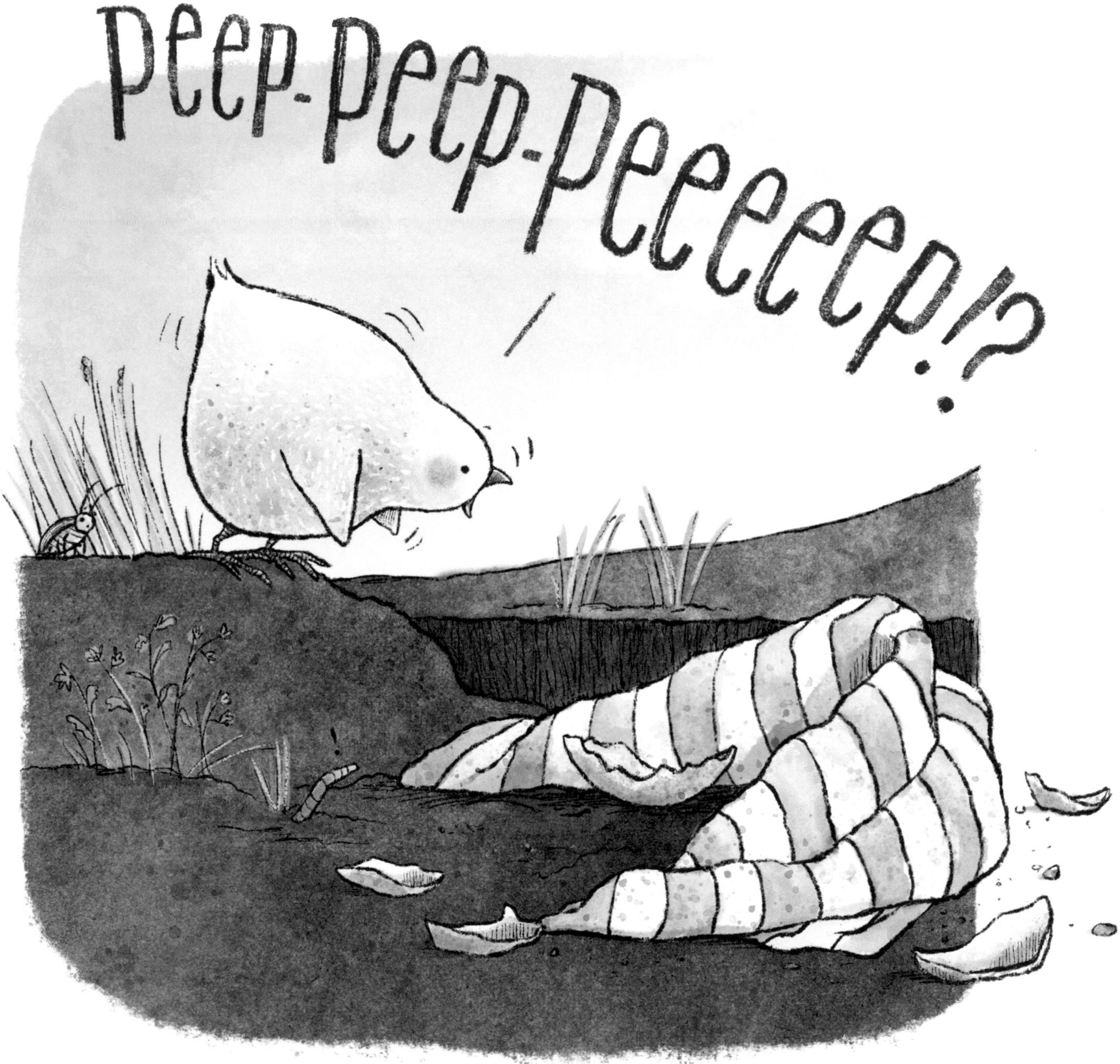
Peep-Peep-Peeeeep!?

Baby Chick's new friend didn't have
a lot to say . . .

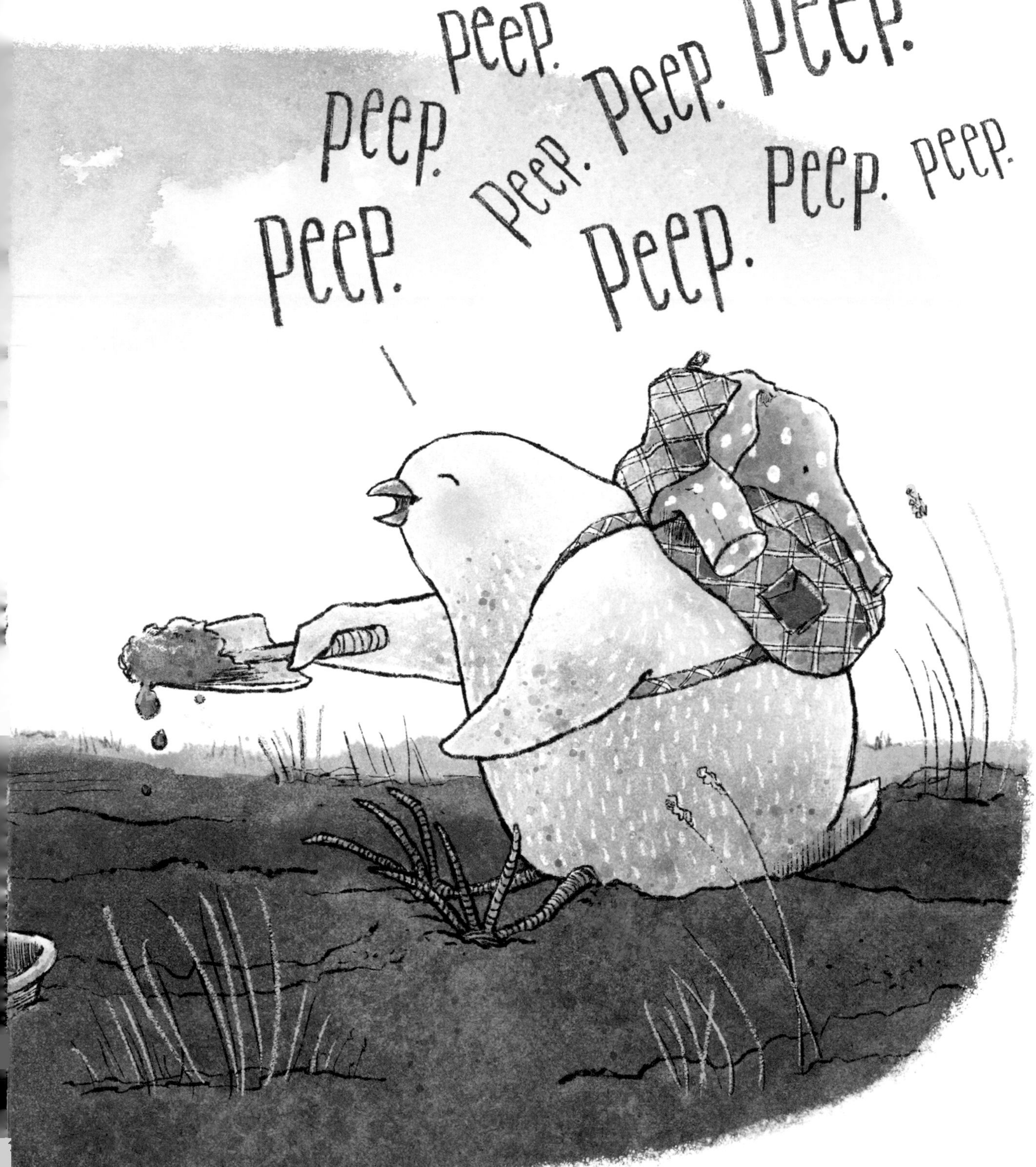
Peep.
Peep.
Peep.
Peep.
Peep.
Peep.
Peep.
Peep.
Peep.

... and that was perfectly okay.

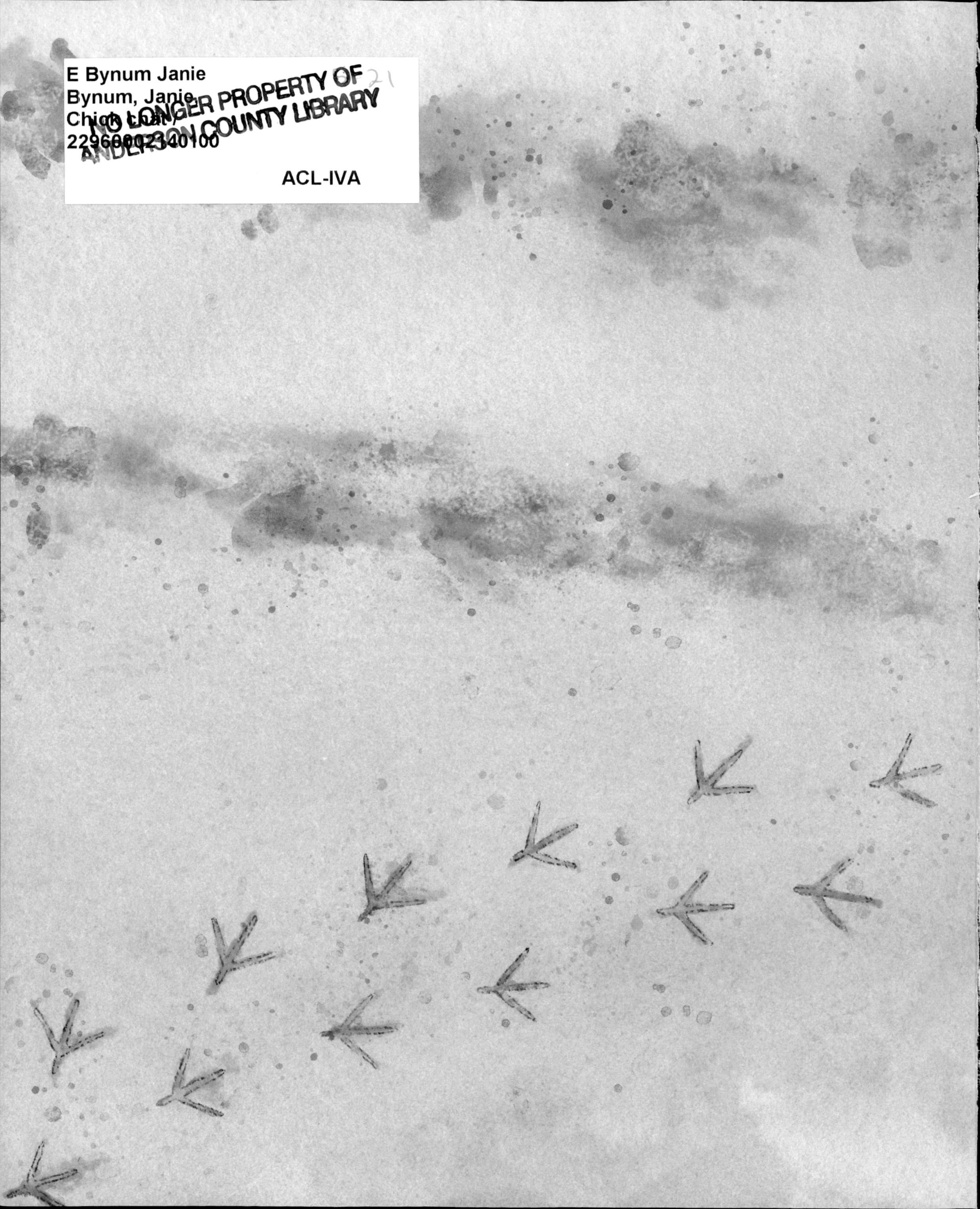